LITTLE LIBRARY

Cinderella

AND OTHER STORIES

Retold by Margaret Carter
Illustrated by Hilda Offen

Kingfisher Books

NEW YORK

KINGFISHER BOOKS
Grisewood & Dempsey Inc.
95 Madison Avenue
New York, New York 10016

First American edition 1994
2 4 6 8 10 9 7 5 3 1
Copyright © Grisewood & Dempsey Ltd. 1993

Library of Congress Cataloging-in-Publication Data
Carter, Margaret.
Cinderella and other stories / retold by Margaret
Carter; illustrated by Hilda Offen,
        p.   cm. — (Little library)
Contents: Cinderella — The princess and the pea —
Aladdin and his wonderful lamp.
1. Fairy tales. [1. Fairy tales. 2. Folklore.] I. Offen,
Hilda, ill. II. Title. III. Series: Little library (New York,
N.Y.)
PZ8.C248C1   1993
398.21—dc20
    [E]   93–5770   CIP   AC
ISBN 1-85697-968-7

Designed by The Pinpoint Design Company
Printed in Great Britain

Contents

Cinderella 9

The Princess and
the Pea 19

Aladdin and
his Wonderful
Lamp 23

Cinderella

Charles Perrault

Once upon a time there were three sisters—two older ones, not very pretty, not very nice—and the youngest, who was both pretty and nice.

The two older girls were jealous of their pretty young sister, and so they made her do all the work. "Light the fire! Hurry up there!" and so on.

By evening the poor girl was so worn out that she'd just sit by the fire to rest.

"You're always sitting in the cinders," said the sisters. "That's what we'll have to call you—Cinders, Cinderella!"

Now the king and queen of the country were giving a big party for their only son, hoping to find a bride for him. Invitations were sent out, and what excitement there was when one came for the sisters!

"We must have new clothes, new shoes," they cried. "Oh, we shall both look so delightful the prince will surely want to marry one of us."

"May I come to the ball?" asked Cinderella. "No!" said the sisters. And that was that.

On the day of the party the sisters took ages to get ready.

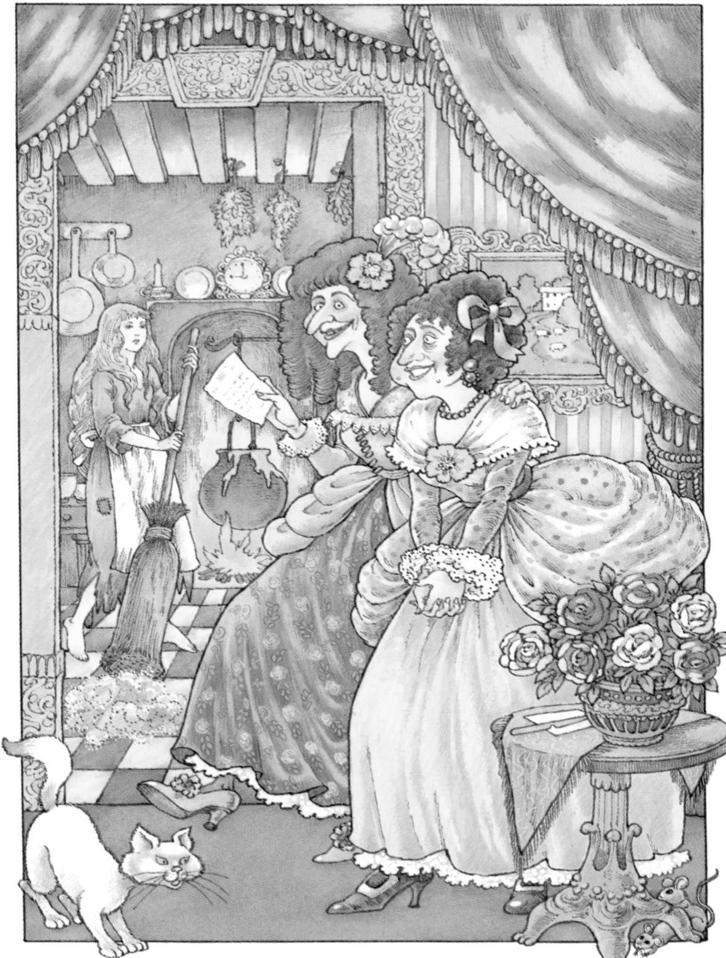

They changed their clothes, lost their shoes, tried on different wigs, gloves—you've never seen such a hullabaloo in your life.

At last they were ready, and off they went, leaving poor Cinderella all by herself.

Sitting alone by the fireside, poor Cinderella felt very sad indeed. One big tear rolled down her cheek and fell into the ashes, plop!

"Don't cry," said a gentle voice, and there was a most beautiful lady.

"I'm your fairy godmother," she said, "and I know you want to go to the ball. And so you shall."

"But I have no coach," said the girl, "no horses, no fine clothes."

The fairy smiled. "Bring me a

pumpkin from the garden," she said.

Cinderella brought the pumpkin. The fairy gave it just one tap of her wand—and there was a coach, golden and shining.

"Now," said the fairy, "bring me the cage of mice you'll find in the kitchen."

She waved her wand again, and instead of six little mice there were six plump horses ready to pull the coach.

In the same way a rat became a fine coachman, and two lizards were changed into footmen.

"You must have a dress," said the fairy, and again she waved her wand—and there stood Cinderella in a most beautiful dress. On her feet were tiny glass slippers.

14

"But remember, Cinderella, the magic stops at midnight. You must leave the ball before the clock strikes."

When Cinderella arrived at the ball everyone wanted to know who this lovely stranger was. The prince danced with her all evening, and the

girl had never been so happy.... And then, suddenly, the clock began to strike twelve! With a cry of alarm Cinderella ran from the palace, but as she did so she dropped one of her slippers.

The prince ran out after her, but she had vanished. He picked up the glass slipper. "I will marry the girl this shoe fits," he declared.

They searched for days. Tall girls, short girls, fair girls, dark girls, all lined up to try on the slipper. But not one did it fit, until they tried the three sisters. For the first it was too narrow, for the second too tight.

"May I try?" asked Cinderella, and it fitted! At that moment the fairy appeared and with one wave of her wand changed the girl's rags into a ball gown. The prince was delighted to find her again, and they were married in no time. So it all ended happily.

The Princess
and the Pea

Hans Christian Andersen

There was once a prince who wanted to marry a real princess, but although he searched he couldn't find one he liked. He came home feeling sad.

One night there was a great storm—thunder, rain, lightning—and in the middle of it all there was a knock at the castle door.

"Who can that be?" asked the king.

Outside stood a young girl, soaking wet, sniffling, and shivering.

"What are you doing out on a night like this?" asked the king.

"I'm a princess," said the girl. "But I've lost my way."

"She doesn't look like a real princess," thought the queen. "We'll soon see about that!"

So while the girl was taking a hot bath, the queen piled twenty quilts and twenty mattresses on a bed. But underneath the first one she put a small, hard pea. The bed was now so high that the princess had to climb a ladder to get to the top, and was quite out of breath when she got there.

"Sleep well," said the queen, smiling to herself.

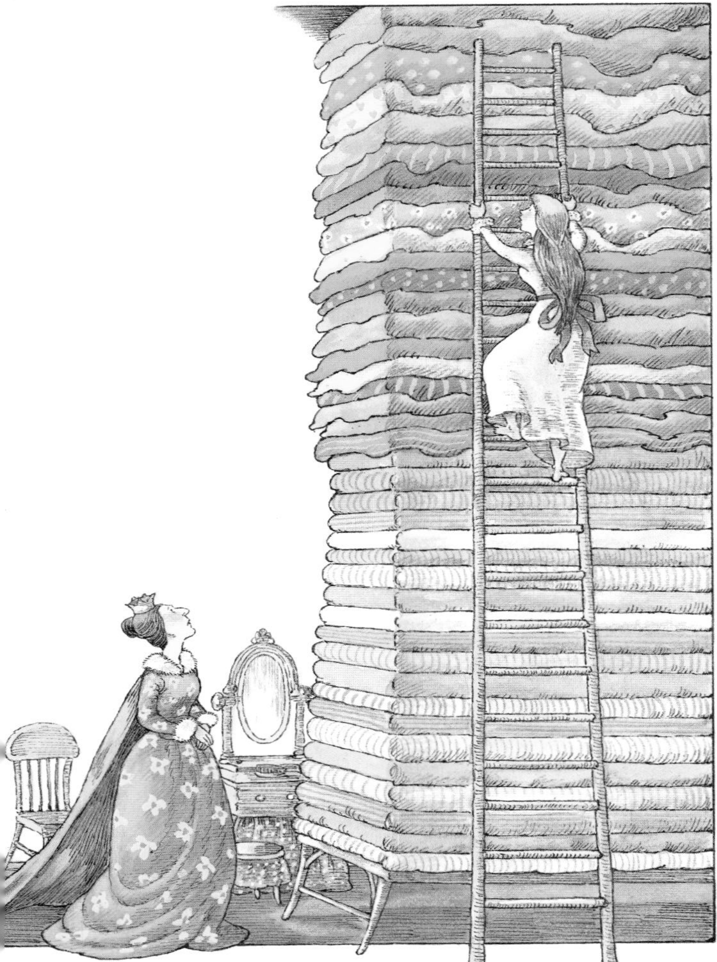

Next morning the princess was the last one to come to breakfast. She looked terrible. "Didn't you sleep well, my dear?" asked the king.

"You're very kind," she yawned, "but there was such a lump in the bed!"

"Aha," said the queen, "only the soft skin of a real princess would have felt that pea through all the quilts and mattresses!"

The prince was delighted to have found a real princess, and after the wedding he put the pea in a glass case in the town museum for all to see.

Aladdin and his Wonderful Lamp

Arabian Nights

Far, far away in the land of China, a boy was playing with his friends. Up and down the streets of the city they ran, too busy to notice that they were being watched by a tall, bearded stranger. At last he spoke to one of them. "Would you help me find something I've lost?" he said. "I'll pay you well for your trouble."

The stranger showed the boy, whose name was Aladdin, a big slab of stone set in the ground. In the middle of the stone was an iron ring.

"Lift the stone," said the stranger, who was really a magician, "and you will find a cave leading to a garden. At the end of the garden is a lamp. Bring the lamp to me and I'll give you many gifts. And here is a ring to show I will keep my promise."

Aladdin put the ring on his finger and climbed into the cave. He soon found the lamp, and on his way back he picked some fruit in the garden.

The magician was waiting for him. "Quick, give me the lamp," he cried. "Help me up first," said Aladdin. "The lamp!" shouted the man, and as they struggled with each other, the stone fell back into place.

Aladdin was trapped in the cave!

The magician, now that his plan had failed, ran away as fast as he could.

"How can I escape?" thought the boy. Still wearing the magician's ring, he wrung his hands in distress. Suddenly, flash! there was an enormous genie, bowing and smiling. "I am the genie of the ring," he said. "What is your command, Master?"

"I'd like to go home, please," said Aladdin very politely.

Next moment he was at home, and his mother was admiring the lamp he'd brought.

"Aladdin," she said, "we could sell this lamp. I'll just rub it a little to make it shine...."

No sooner had she rubbed the lamp than whoosh! there stood another genie!

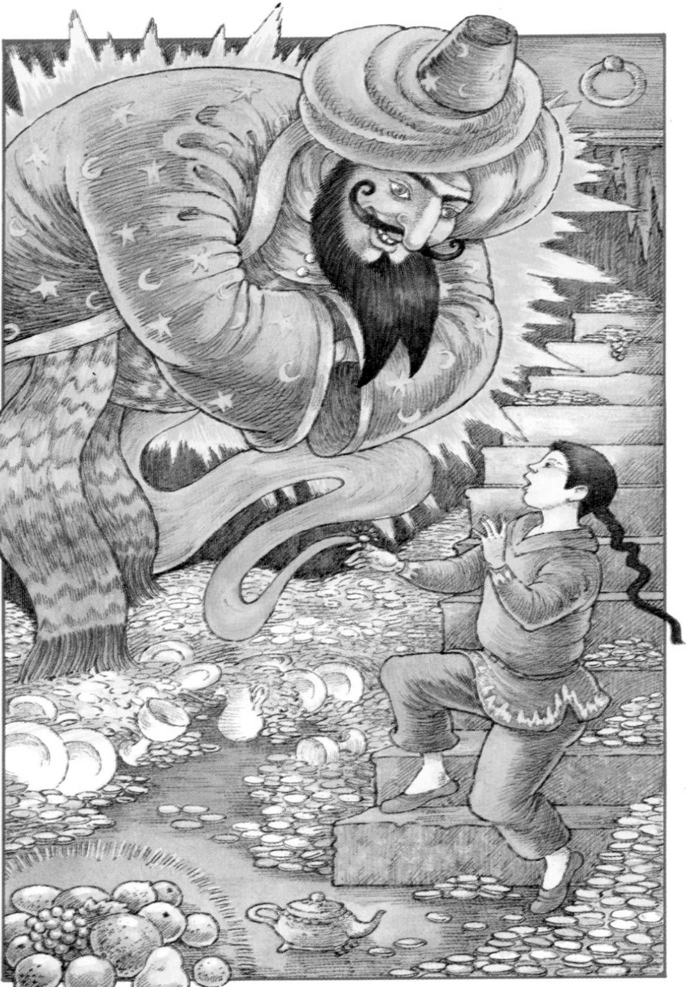

"I am the genie of the lamp," he said. "Your wish is my command!"

"We'd like some food," said Aladdin, "and nice clothes and a better house." And there it all was!

"Anything else?" asked the genie.

"Yes," said Aladdin, "I'd like to marry the Sultan's daughter!"

"Take her the fruit," said the

genie—and vanished.

As soon as the Sultan saw the fruit he realized they were precious jewels. "This man would make a good husband," he thought. "Could you build her a palace?" he asked.

"No problem," said Aladdin, and by the next day there it was, with a red carpet for the princess to walk on to her new home—all thanks to the genie of the lamp.

LITTLE LIBRARY

Red Books to collect:

Beauty and the Beast
and Other Stories

▲

Cinderella
and Other Stories

▲

Goldilocks
and Other Stories

▲

Little Red Riding Hood
and Other Stories

The Pumpkin Mystery

by **Carol Wallace**

illustrated by

Steve Björkman

SCHOLASTIC INC.
New York Toronto London Auckland
Sydney Mexico City New Delhi Hong Kong

To Keegan Keith Wallace
C. W.

For Sonora and Shad
S. B.

ISBN 978-0-545-49014-6

12 11 10 9 8 7 6 5 4   14 15 16 17/0

Printed in the U.S.A.   40

First Scholastic printing, September 2012

Contents

1. *Too Early for Pumpkins*   4

2. *Keep the Rabbits Out!*   12

3. *Where Are the Pumpkins?*   22

4. *The Surprise*   31

Chapter 1

Too Early for Pumpkins

"What's going on out there, Mocha?"
asked Scruffy.

The cat rubbed against Mocha.

The two friends watched
through the fence.

Daddy opened the gate.

"Let's get the garden started,"
he said.

Scruffy's tail flipped as
he followed Mocha.
"Are you ready to get to work?"
Daddy asked Aden and Leah.
"Dad, can we plant pumpkins again?"

"Sure, but it's a little early,"
  said Daddy.
"Do you want them
  for Halloween?"
"Yes!" Leah and Aden shouted.
"Pumpkins take about 120 days
  to grow," Dad said.
"We need to wait until June."

"It was fun throwing the leftover
pumpkins into the pasture."
Aden smiled.
"You and your pals made a
huge mess," Mama said.

Mocha rubbed her head
against Aden's hand.
"We need to get the ground ready
for beans and corn today," said Dad.
"Hey, where are the stakes?"
Mom called from the shed.

Mocha ran to the shed.

"Steak! I love steak."

She sniffed and sniffed.

"Do you smell steak?" Mocha asked.

"They didn't mean food,"
Scruffy said.

"Mama is looking for wood things."

"Why?" Mocha perked her ears.

"First they put the stakes
in the ground.
Next they stretch string
between them.
Then they have
a line to follow
for planting."

"Come on, Mocha, you can help dig!"
Mama scooped up Scruffy.
She put him in the wheelbarrow.
Mama pushed the cat to the garden.

Daddy walked behind the noisy tiller.
Dirt rolled from the metal tines.
"Want to dig for gophers?"
Scruffy invited.
"No thanks, I want to dig in
this nice, soft dirt."
The more Dad tilled the ground,
the more Mocha dug.

Dirt flew.

"Mocha! Stop digging!"
Daddy finally ordered.

"But this is fun," Mocha said.

"Mocha!" Daddy shouted again.

Chapter 2
Keep the Rabbits Out!

Daddy and Mama raked the dirt.

Aden and Leah counted the stakes.

Daddy pounded stakes
into the ground.

Mama stretched the string.

"It looks good!"

They all piled the soil
along the string.

Daddy and Mama poked holes
in the ridge of dirt.
Aden and Leah dropped seeds
in each hole.

Finally, Daddy covered
the seeds with soil.
Mama pulled the water hose
from the yard.
"Aden! Leah! Come water
the garden."

"So, what do we do next?"
Aden asked.

"We have to keep the weeds out,"
Mama said.

"Mocha will keep the rabbits out,"
said Daddy.

Mocha's ears perked. "I love to
chase rabbits."

When the tiny plants began to grow,
the rabbits started visiting
the garden.

"Stay away," Mocha growled.
"You're behind the fence.
You can't get us, Mocha Dog,"
said the rabbits.
Louie Rabbit nibbled
the tender plants.
Mocha barked and barked.

"Need some help, Mocha?"
Scruffy meowed.
The cat jumped from the tree.
"Run, rabbits," Scruffy said.
The rabbits ran from the garden.
Mama and Daddy worked
in the garden every day.

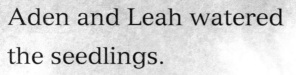

Aden and Leah watered
the seedlings.
Warm days brought more and
more tiny plants.
The beans in the garden
were up to Aden's knees.
The corn was higher
than Daddy's waist.

"Is it time to plant pumpkins yet?"
Aden asked.

"Sure, we'll soak the seeds in water.
That will give them a head start,"
Dad said.

Dad was up early working
on the tiller.
Aden pulled some big weeds.
Mocha and Scruffy sniffed the field.
The rabbits hid.

"We have to pile the dirt up," Dad said.
"We put five or six seeds
  in each mound."
  Mocha started digging.
  Aden and Leah piled dirt
  to make little hills.
  Daddy followed behind them.

He dropped seeds in the mounds.
Mama put dirt over them.
Mocha and Scruffy sniffed
the edge of the field.
"We'll let nature work," Daddy said.

Chapter 3

Where Are the Pumpkins?

"Are there any pumpkins?"
Leah asked.
"We *should* have some sprouts."
Daddy knelt down and dug
in the soil.
"Seeds are still here. No sprouts yet,"
Daddy said.
"Maybe they need more water."

Aden watered each mound.
"We may have to replant
the pumpkins.
The rest of the garden looks great."

A few weeks later
Mocha and Scruffy
followed Daddy and Mama.
Daddy stared at
the garden.

"What's happening to
our pumpkins?
We only have a few plants."
Mama put her hands on her hips.
"There are even fewer blossoms."
"It just doesn't make sense,"
Daddy said.

"I wanted another pumpkin party,"
Aden said.
"Everyone had a pumpkin
to decorate."

"I was going
to make a
princess one,"
Leah whined.
"We can **buy**
some pumpkins,"
Daddy said.
"It was fun to
have our friends
pick their own from the garden.
That was the best part," Leah said.
Aden sat down.
"The pumpkin
toss was the
best part,"
he said.

The leaves were beginning
to turn their fall colors.
Scruffy spotted Mocha
in her doghouse.
"Mocha, why are you moping?"
Scruffy asked.
"Leah and Aden are sad.
I wish they had some pumpkins.

Where are the pumpkins?"
Mocha whined.

"I just saw two pumpkins,"
Scruffy said.

"There are only five plants, and
the pumpkins are too small
and too green," said Mocha.

"The Mouse family got them,"
a quiet voice said.

"Who said that?" Mocha yipped.

"I've got some information for you."
The dog jumped up.

Louie Rabbit was standing
by the fence.

Mocha stepped closer.
"The rain washed some of
the seeds away.
Most of the others rotted.
There was too much water."
"How do you know?" Scruffy asked.
"Robbie, the baby mouse, told me.
He said his dad ate some
and got sick.

I can help you with your problem,
but we have to make a deal."
Scruffy and Mocha stared
at each other.
"What kind of deal?" Mocha asked.
"If you're looking for pumpkins,
meet me by the pecan tree in
the pasture."
The rabbit ran toward the barn.

Chapter 4

The Surprise

"Start barking. Mama will let
you out," said Scruffy.
Mocha barked and barked.
Mama came to the door.
"You need a run, Mocha?"
As soon as Mama opened the gate,
Mocha ran to the big tree.
Scruffy trotted behind him.

Louie was nibbling grass.
"We need to talk first," he said.

"What is it?" Scruffy asked.
"When your family starts
planting the garden in the spring,
we need some garden time."

"My job is to keep rabbits *out!*"
Mocha said.

"We don't want it all.
Your people plant a lot of seeds.
Then they thin out the rows.
We can take care of those
extra plants," Louie said.

"We can do that," Mocha yipped.

"Do you promise?" Louie asked.

"Yes," Scruffy and Mocha
said together.

"Okay. Follow me."
Mocha and Scruffy followed
Louie to the field.
"Look behind these bushes."
Louie scooted under the plant.
The dog and the cat shoved
through the bushes.
"Wow! How did you do this?"
Scruffy asked.
"I didn't do it. I just found it,"
Louie said.
"We'll be back!"
Mocha nudged
Scruffy.

When Mama opened the garden gate,
Mocha and Scruffy ran to the pasture.
Mocha barked as loud as she could.
"What's up with them?"
Daddy asked.

Aden ran after the dog and the cat.

"Mocha is barking at the bushes."

"Maybe it's an armadillo," Leah said.

"Or a skunk," Mama warned.

Mocha poked her nose
into the brush pile.
Scruffy shoved
his way into
the bushes.

"What is it?"
Aden asked.
Daddy pushed
back the limbs.

"Look at that!" Daddy said.

"PUMPKINS!" Mama, Aden,
  and Leah cried.

"How many do you see?"
  Daddy asked.

"One, four, seven, nineteen . . . ,"
  Leah counted.

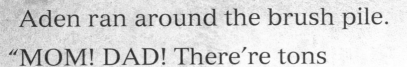

Aden ran around the brush pile.
"MOM! DAD! There're tons
of pumpkins!"
"We can have our pumpkin party!"
Aden said.
"Where did these pumpkins
come from?"
Daddy scratched his head.

"We had the pumpkin toss here!"
said Aden.
"I guess we need to have
another pumpkin throw
in the pasture," Mama said.
"Mocha saved the day!"
Leah cheered.

Mocha and Scruffy looked behind
the clump of grass.
Louie was watching.
Scruffy purred.
Mocha wagged her tail.
Louie just wiggled his nose.